This Book Belongs to:

_____

To Sonja and Michael, whose hearts
are as big as an elephant's.

ISBN: 978-1-912497-16-4
www.flyingeyebooks.com

Reza Dalvand

Mrs Bibi's Elephant

Flying Eye Books
London | New York

Mrs Bibi had a very big pet elephant.

Every day, they went out
for a walk together.

In the morning, they
played with the children
in the street...

...and in the afternoon,
they had tea and cake.

At night, Mrs Bibi told her elephant stories
so that he would have nice dreams.

But the townspeople didn't like Mrs Bibi's elephant.

They thought he was too big and too loud...

...and caused too many traffic jams.

They didn't understand why anyone would want a pet.
They just cause trouble!

The townspeople believed that homes should be filled with beautiful objects like chandeliers and jewellery.

They said that instead of talking to an elephant,
Mrs Bibi should read the newspaper, check the stock market
and keep up to date with economics!

But Mrs Bibi didn't own any fancy objects ...
nor was she interested in checking the stock market
or reading about economics.

She was at her happiest being with her elephant,
speaking about the past and laughing.

The townspeople protested for the elephant to leave.
They were afraid that their children might also want pets one day.

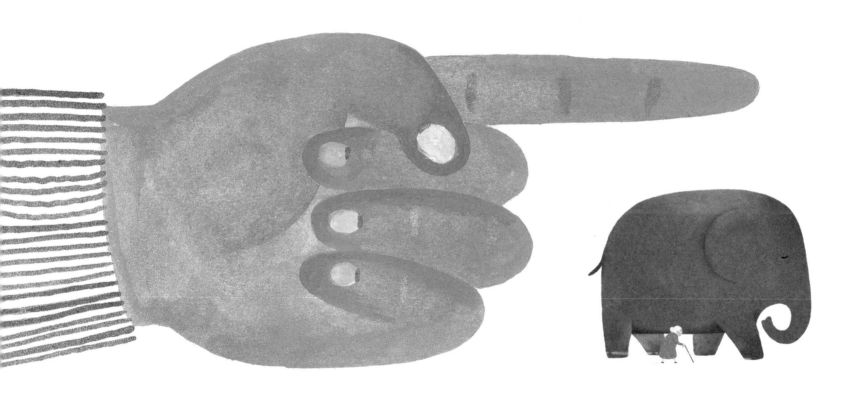

The town judge ordered that the elephant be taken
to the zoo the very next morning.

Mrs Bibi was very sad that night.
She hugged her elephant and told
him stories until he fell asleep.

She had to do something to stop them
from taking her elephant away.

The next day, when the townspeople came to Mrs Bibi's house to take her elephant, there was no one there.

They looked all over the town, but it was no use.
Mrs Bibi and her gigantic elephant were nowhere to be found...

After Mrs Bibi and her elephant left,
the town wasn't the same.

The children
stopped
playing in
the street...

...people
stopped
smiling...

...and everyone
felt as if
something
was missing.

A great sense of longing
filled the elephant's place
in the children's hearts.

The townspeople didn't know what to do.
They realised how much happier the place was
when Mrs Bibi and her elephant were around.

So, they decided to make a change.

The children would get their own pets and bring life back into their town.

Some of the children
picked dogs and
others picked cats.

Some even found
their own elephants.

Everyone learned that home is more than
just a place for fancy objects and economics.
It's a place for living.

A place for those who might even have
room for huge elephants in their hearts.
Because Mrs Bibi and her elephant weren't gone.

Not really.